THE WORSHIPPER
OF THE IMAGE

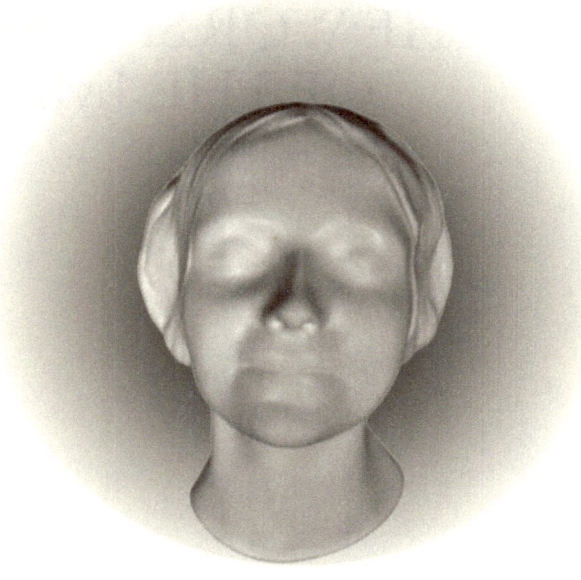

L'Inconnue de la Seine, a purported death-mask, which became immensely popular in the late nineteenth century, and which likely provided the author with inspiration for this piece.

THE WORSHIPPER OF THE IMAGE

by

RICHARD LE GALLIENNE

SANDNESS
MICHAEL WALMER
2025

The Worshipper of the Image first published 1900

This edition published 2025 by

Michael Walmer
Little Pradies
13a Melby
Sandness
Shetland ZE2 9PL

ISBN 978-1-7638700-0-0 paperback

TO SILENCIEUX

THIS TRAGIC FAIRY-TALE

Contents

The Worshipper of the Image

🎋

CHAPTER I

SMILING SILENCE

Evening was in the wood, still as the dreaming bracken, secretive, moving softly among the pines as a young witch gathering simples. She wore a hood of finely woven shadows, yet, though she drew it close, sunbeams trooping westward flashed strange lights across her haunted face.

The birds that lived in the wood had broken out into sudden singing as she stole in, hungry for silence, passionate to be alone; and at the foot of every tree she cried " Hush ! Hush ! " to the bed-time nests. When all but one were still, she slipped the hood from her face and listened to her own bird, the night-jar, toiling at his hopeless love from a bough on which already hung a little star.

Then it was that a young man, with a face shining with sorrow, vaulted lightly over the mossed fence and dipped down the green path, among the shadows and the toadstools and the silence.

"Silencieux," he said over to himself —"I love you, Silencieux."

Far down the wood came and went through the trees the black and white gable of a little châlet to which he was dreaming his way.

Suddenly a small bronze object caught his eye moving across the mossy path. It was a beautiful beetle, very slim and graceful in shape, with singularly long and fine antennæ. Antony had loved these things since he was a child, — dragonflies with their lamp-like eyes of luminous horn, moths with pall-like wings

that filled the world with silence as you
looked at them, sleepy as death — loved
them with the passion of a Japanese artist
who delights to carve them on quaint
nuggets of metal. Perhaps it was that
they were so like words — words to which
he had given all the love and worship of
his life. Surely he had loved Silencieux [1]
more since he had found for her that
beautiful name.

He held the beetle in his hand a long
while, loving it. Then he said to himself,
with a smile in which was the delight of a
success: " A vase-shaped beetle with deer's
horns."

The phrase delighted him. He set the
insect down on the path, tenderly. He
had done with it. He had carved it in
seven words. The little model might

---

[1] Of course, the writer is aware that while " Silencieux " is feminine, her name is masculine. In such
fanciful names, however, such license has always been
considered allowable.

now touch its delicate way among the ferns at peace.

"A vase-shaped beetle with deer's horns," he repeated as he walked on, and then the gathering gloom of the wood suggested an addition: "And some day I shall find in the wood that moth of which I have dreamed since childhood — the dark moth with the face of death between his wings."

The châlet stood on a little clearing, in a little circle of pines. From it the ground sloped down towards the valley, and at some distance beneath smoke curled from a house lost amid clouds of foliage, the abounding green life of this damp and brooding hollow. A great window looking down the woodside filled one side of the châlet, and the others were dark with books, an occasional picture or figured jar lighting up the shadow. A small fire flickered beneath a quaintly devised mantel, though it was summer — for the mists crept up the hill at night and chilled the souls of the books. A great old bureau, with a wonderful belly of mahogany, filled a corner of the room, breathing antique mystery and refinement. At one end of it, on a small vacant space of wall, hung a cast, apparently the death-mask of a woman, by which the eye was immediately attracted with something of a shock and held by a curious fascination. The face was smiling, a smile of great peace, and also of a strange cunning. One other characteristic it had : the woman looked as though at any moment she would suddenly open her eyes, and if you turned away from her and looked again, she seemed to be smiling to herself because she had opened them that moment behind your back, and just closed them again in time.

It was a face that never changed and yet was always changing.

She looked doubly strange in the evening light, and her smile softened and deepened as the shadows gathered in the room.

Antony came and stood in front of her.

"Silencieux," he whispered, "I love you, Silencieux. Smiling Silence, I love you. All day long on the moors your smile has stolen like a moonbeam by my side — "

As he spoke, from far down the wood came the gentle sound of a woman's voice calling "Antony," and coming nearer as it called.

With a shade of impatience, Antony bent nearer to the image and kissed it.

"Good-bye, Silencieux," he whispered, "Good-bye, until the rising of the moon."

Then he passed out on to the little staircase that led down into the wood, and called back to the approaching voice : "I am coming, Beatrice," — 'Beatrice' being the name of his wife.

As he called, a shaft of late sunlight suddenly irradiated the tall slim form of a woman coming up the wood. She wore no hat, and the sun made a misty glory of her pale gold hair. She seemed a fairy romantic thing thus gliding in her yellow silk gown through the darkening pines. And her face was the face of the image, feature for feature. There was on it too the same light, the same smile.

" Antony," she called, as they drew nearer to each other, " where in the wide world have you been? Dinner has been waiting for half-an-hour."

" Dinner !" he said, laughing, and kissing her kindly. " Fancy! the High Muses have made me half-an-hour late for dinner. Beauty has made me forget my dinner. Disgraceful ! "

" I don't mind your forgetting dinner, Antony — but you might have remembered me."

" Do you think I could remember

Beauty and forget you? Yes! you *are* beautiful to-night, Silen — Beatrice. You look like a lady one meets walking by a haunted well in some old Arthurian tale."

"Hush!" said Beatrice, "listen to the night-jar. He is worth a hundred night-ingales."

"Yes; what a passion is that!" said Antony, "so sincere, and yet so fasci-nating too."

"'Yet,' do you say, Antony? Why, sincerity is the most fascinating thing in the world."

And as they listened, Antony's heart had stolen back to Silencieux, and once more in fancy he pressed his lips to hers in the dusk: "It is with such an eternal passion that I love you, Silencieux."

CHAPTER II

THE COMING OF SILENCIEUX

THE manner in which Antony had found and come to love Silencieux was a strange illustration of that law by which one love grows out of another — that law by which men love living women because of the dead, and dead women because of the living.

One day as chance had sent him, picking his way among the orange boxes, the moving farms, and the wig-makers of Covent Garden, he had come upon a sculptor's shop, oddly crowded in among Cockney carters and decaying vegetables. Faces of Greece and Rome gazed at him suddenly from a broad window, and for a few moments he forsook the motley beauty of modern London for the ordered loveliness of antiquity.

Through white corridors of faces he passed, with the cold breath of classic art upon his cheek, and in the company of the dead who live for ever he was conscious of a contagion of immortality.

Soon in an alcove of faces he grew conscious of a presence. Some one was smiling near him. He turned, and, almost with a start, found that — as he then thought — it was no living thing, but just a plaster cast among the others, that was thus shining, like a star among the dead. A face not ancient, not modern ; but a face of yesterday, to-day, and for ever.

Instantly he knew he had seen the face before. Where ?

Why, of course, it was the face of Beatrice, feature for feature. How strange ! — and, loving Beatrice, he bought it, because of his great love for her ! Who was

the artist, what the time and circumstance,
that had anticipated in this strange fashion
the only face he had ever really loved on
earth ?

He sought information of the shop-
keeper, who told him a strange little
story of an unknown model and an unknown artist, and two tragic fates.

When Antony had brought Silencieux
home to Beatrice, she had at first taken
that delight in her which every created
thing takes in a perfect, or even an imper-
fect, reflection of itself. To have been
anticipated in a manner so unusual gave
back in romantic suggestiveness what at
first sight it seemed to steal from one's
personal originality. Only at first sight —
for, if like Beatrice, you were the possessor
of a face so uncommon in type that your
lover might, with little fear of disproof,
declare, at all events in England, that
there was none other like it, you might
grow superstitious as you looked at an

anticipation so creepily identical, and conceive strange fancies of re-incarnation. What if this had been you in some former existence! Or at all events, if there is any truth in those who tell us that in the mould and lines of our faces and hands — yes! and in every secret marking of our bodies — our fates are written as in a parchment; would it not be reasonable to surmise, perhaps to fear, that the writing should mean the same on one face as on the other, and the fates as well as the faces prove identical?

Beatrice gave the mask back to Antony, with a little shiver.

"It is very wonderful, very strange, but she makes me frightened. What was the story the man told you, Antony?"

"No doubt it was all nonsense," Antony replied, "but he said that it was the death-mask of an unknown girl found drowned in the Seine."

"Drowned in the Seine!" exclaimed

Beatrice, growing almost as white as the image.

"Yes! and he said too that the story went that the sculptor who moulded it had fallen so in love with the dead girl, that he had gone mad and drowned himself in the Seine also."

"Can it be true, Antony?"

"I hope so, for it is so beautiful, — and nothing is really beautiful till it has come true."

"But the pain, the pity of it — Antony."

"That is a part of the beauty,' surely — the very essence of its beauty — "

"Beauty! beauty! O Antony, that is always your cry. I can only think of the terror, the human anguish. Poor girl — " and she turned again to the image as it lay upon the table, — "see how the hair lies moulded round her ears with the water, and how her eyelashes stick to her cheek — Poor girl."

" But see how happy she looks.   Why should we pity one who can smile like that ?   See how peaceful she looks ; " and with a sudden whim, Antony took the image and set it lying back on a soft cushion in a corner of the couch, at the same time throwing round its neck his black cloak, which he had cast off as be came in.

The image nestled into the cushion as though it had veritably been a living woman weary for sleep, and softly smiling that it was near at last.   So comfortable she seemed, you could have sworn she breathed.

Antony lifted her head once or twice with his fingers, to delight himself with seeing her sink back luxuriously once more.

Beatrice grew more and more white.

" Antony, please stop.   I cannot bear it.   She looks so terribly alive."

At that moment Antony's touch had been a little too forcible, the image hung poised for a moment and then began to fall in the direction of Beatrice.

"Oh, she is falling," she almost screamed, as Antony saved the cast from the floor. "For God's sake, stop!"

"How childish of you, Beatrice. She is only plaster. I never knew you such a baby."

"I cannot help it, Antony. I know it is foolish, but I cannot help it. I think living in this place has made me morbid. She seems so alive — so evil, so cruel. I am sorry you bought her, Antony. I cannot bear to look at her. Won't you take her away? Take her up into the wood. Keep her there. Take her now. I shall not be able to sleep all night if I know she is in the house."

She was half hysterical, and Antony soothed her gently.

"Yes, yes, dear. I'm sorry. I'll take her up the wood now this minute. Wait till I light the lantern. Poor Beatrice, I

never dreamed she would affect you so.
I loved her, dear — because I love you;
but I would rather break her in pieces
than that she should make you unhappy.
Though to break any image of you, dear,"
he added tenderly, " would seem a kind
of sacrilege.   You know how I love you,
Beatrice, don't you ? "

" Of course I do, dear; and it was
sweet of you to buy her for my sake,
and I 'm quite silly to-night.   To-morrow I shall think nothing about her.
Still, dear, she does frighten me, I can't
tell why.   There seems something malignant about her, something that threatens
our happiness.   Oh, how silly I am — "

Meanwhile, Antony had lit an old brass
lantern, and presently he was flashing his
way up among the dark sounds of the
black old wood, with that ghostly face
tenderly pressed against his side.

He stopped once to turn his lantern
upon her.   How mysterious she looked,
here in the night, under the dark pines !

He too felt a little haunted as he climbed his châlet staircase and unlocked the door, every sound he made echoing fatefully in the silent wood ; and when he had found a place for the image and hung her there, she certainly looked a ghostly companion for the midnight lamp, in the middle of a wood.

How strangely she smiled, the smile almost of one taking possession.

No wonder Beatrice had been frightened. Was there some mysterious life in the thing, after all ? Why should these indefinite forebodings come over him as he looked at her ! — But he was growing as childish as Beatrice. Surely midnight, a dark wood, a lantern, and a death-mask, with two owls whistling to each other across the valley, were enough to account for any number of forebodings ! But Antony shivered, for all that, as he locked the door and hastened back again down the wood.

CHAPTER III

THE NORTHERN SPHINX

ANTONY had not written a poem to his wife since their little girl Wonder had been born, now some four years ago. Surely it was from no lack of love, this silence, but merely due to the working of what would seem to be a law of the artistic temperament : that to turn a muse into a wife, however long and faithfully loved, is to bid good-bye to the muse. But a day or two after the coming of Silencieux, Antony found himself suddenly inspired once more to sing of his wife. It was the best poem he had written for a long time, and when it was finished, he came down the wood impatient to read it to Beatrice. This was the poem, which he called " The Northern Sphinx " : —

Sphinx of the North, with subtler smile
   Than hers who in the yellow South,
   With make-believe mysterious mouth,
Deepens the *ennui* of the Nile ;

And, with no secret left to tell,
   A worn and withered old coquette,
   Dreams sadly that she draws us yet,
With antiquated charm and spell :

Tell me your secret, Sphinx, — for mine ! —
   What means the colour of your eyes,
   Half innocent and all so wise,
Blue as the smoke whose wavering line

Curls upward from the sacred pyre
   Of sacrifice or holy death,
   Pale twisting wreaths of opal breath,
From fire mounting into fire.

What is the meaning of your hair ?
   That little fairy palace wrought
   With many a grave fantastic thought ;
I send a kiss to wander there,

To climb from golden stair to stair,
   Wind in and out its cunning bowers, —
   O garden gold with golden flowers,
O little palace built of hair !

The meaning of your mouth, who knows?
   O mouth, where many meanings meet —
   Death kissed it stern, Love kissed it sweet,
And each has shaped its mystic rose.

Mouth of all sweets, whose sweetness sips
   Its tribute honey from all hives,
   The sweetest of the sweetest lives,
Soft flowers and little children's lips;

Yet rather learnt its heavenly smile
   From sorrow, God's divinest art,
   Sorrow that breaks and breaks the heart,
Yet makes a music all the while.

Ah! what is that within your eyes,
   Upon your lips, within your hair,
   The sacred art that makes you fair,
The wisdom that hath made you wise?

Tell me your secret, Sphinx, — for mine! —
   The mystic word that from afar
   God spake and made you rose and star,
The *fiat lux* that bade you shine.

While Antony read, Beatrice's face grew
sadder and sadder. When he had finished
she said: —

"It is very beautiful, Antony — but it is not written for me."

"What can you mean, Beatrice? Who else can it be written for?"

"To the Image of me that you have set up in my place."

"Beatrice, are you going mad?"

"It is quite true, all the same. Time will show. Perhaps you don't know it yourself as yet, but you will before long."

"But, Beatrice, the poem shows its own origin. Has your image blue eyes, or curiously coiled hair —"

"Oh, yes, of course, you thought of me. You filled in from me. But the inspiration, the wish to write it, came from the image —"

"It is certainly true that I love to look at it, as I love to look at a picture of you — because it is you —"

"As yet, no doubt, but you will soon love it for its own sake. You are already beginning."

" I love an image ! You are too ridiculous, Beatrice."

" Does it really seem so strange, dear? I sometimes think you have never loved anything else."

Antony had laughed down Beatrice's fancies, yet all the time she had been talking he was conscious that the idea she had suggested was appealing to him with a perverse fascination.

To love, not the literal beloved, but the purified stainless image of her, — surely this would be to ascend into the region of spiritual love, a love unhampered and untainted by the earth.

As he said this to himself, his mind, ever pitilessly self-conscious, knew it was but a subterfuge, a fine euphemism for a strange desire which he had known was already growing within him; for when Beatrice had spoken of bis loving an image, it was no abstract passion he had conceived, but some fanciful variation of earthly love

— a love of beauty centring itself upon some form midway between life and death, inanimate and yet alive, human and yet removed from the accidents of humanity.

To love an image with one's whole heart! If only one could achieve that — and never come out of the dream.

These thoughts gave him a new desire to look again at the image. He felt that in some way she would be changed, and he hastened up the wood in a strange expectancy.

CHAPTER IV

AT THE RISING OF THE MOON

BUT a week or two more, and Beatrice's prophecy had progressed so far towards fulfilment, that Antony was going about the woods and the moors saying over to himself the name he had found for the Image, as we saw in the first chapter ; and his love for Silencieux, begun more or less as a determined self-illusion, grew more and more of a reality. Every day new life welled into Silencieux's face, as every day life ebbed from the face of Beatrice, surely foreseeing the coming on of what she had feared. For the love he gave to Silencieux Antony must take away from Beatrice, from whom as the days went by he grew more and more withdrawn.

It was true that the long lonely days which he spent in the wood bore fruit in a remarkable productiveness. Never had his imagination been so enkindled, or his pen so winged. But this very industry, the proofs of which he would each evening bring down the wood for that fine judgment of Beatrice's, which, in spite of all, still remained more to him than any other praise — this very industry was the secret confirmation for Beatrice's sad heart. No longer the inspirer, she was yet, she bitterly told herself, honoured among women as a critic. Her heart might bleed, and her eyes fill with tears, as he read ; but then, as he would say, the Beauty, the Music! Is it Beautiful ? Is it Music ? If it be that, no matter how it has been made ! Let us give thanks for creation, though it involves the sacrifice of our own most tender and sacred feelings. To set mere personal feelings against Beauty — human tears against an immortal creation !

Did he spare his own feelings? Indeed he did not.

On the night when we first met him bidding good-bye to Silencieux "until the rising of the moon," he had sat through dinner eating but little, feverishly and somewhat cruelly gay. Though he was as yet too kind to admit it to himself, Beatrice was beginning to bore him, not merely by her sadness, which his absorption prevented his realising except in flashes, but by her very resemblance to the Image — of which, from having been the beloved original, she was, in his eyes, becoming an indifferent materialisation. The sweet flesh he had loved so tenderly became an offence to him, as a medium too gross for the embodiment of so beautiful a face. Such a face as Silencieux's demanded a more celestial porcelain.

Dinner at last finished, he made an excuse to Beatrice for leaving her alone once more at the end as he had during all

the rest of the day, and hastened to keep
his tryst with Silencieux. During dinner
the conscious side of his mind had been
luxuriating in the romantic sound of
" until the rising of the moon," — for he
was as yet a long way from being quite
simple even with Silencieux, — and the
idea of his going out with serious eager-
ness to meet one who, if she was as he
knew a living being, was an image too,
delighted his sense of fantastic make-
believe.

There is in all love that element of
make-believe. Every woman who is loved
is partly the creation of her lover's fancy.
He consciously siderealises her, and with
open eyes magnifies her importance to his
life. Antony but made believe and mag-
nified uncommonly — and his dream of
vivifying white plaster was perhaps less
desperate than the dreams of some, that
would breathe the breath of life into the
colder clay of some beloved woman, who

seems spontaneously to live but is dead all the while.

Silencieux appeared to be dead, but beneath that eternal smile, as Beatrice had divined, as Antony was learning, she was only too terribly alive. Yes! Antony's was the easier dream.

The moon and Antony came up the wood together from opposite ends, and when Antony entered his châlet Silencieux was already waiting for him, her head crowned with a moonbeam. He kissed her softly and took her with him out into the ferns.

CHAPTER V

SILENCIEUX SPEAKS

So long as the moon held, Antony stole up the wood each night to meet Silencieux —"at the rising of the moon." Sometimes he would lie in a hollow with her head upon his knee, and gaze for an hour at a time, entranced, into her face. He would feign to himself that she slept, and he would hold his breath lest he should awaken her. Sometimes he would say in a tender whisper, not loud enough for her to hear : —

"It is cold to-night, Silencieux. See, my cloak will keep you warm."

Once as he did this she heaved a gentle sigh, as though thanking him.

At other times he would place her against the gable of the châlet, so that the moonlight fell upon her, and then he would plunge into the wood and walk its whole length, so that, as he wound his way back through the intervening brakes, her face would come and go, glimmering away off through the leafage, beckoning to him to return. And once he thought he heard her call his name very softly through the wood.

That may have been an illusion, but it was during these days that he did actually hear her speak for the first time. He had been writing till past midnight, with her smile just above him, and when he had turned out the lamp and was moving to the door through the vague flickering light of the fire, he distinctly heard a voice very luxurious and tender say "Antony," just behind him. It was hardly more than a whisper, but its sweetness thrilled his blood, and half in joy and fear he turned to her again. But she was only smiling inscrutably as before, and she spoke no more for that night.

CHAPTER VI

THE THREE BLACK PONDS

At the bottom of the valley, approached by sunken honeysuckle lanes that seemed winding into the centre of the earth, lay three black ponds, almost hidden in a *cul-de-sac* of woodland. Though long since appropriated by nature, made her own by moss and rooted oaks, they were so set one below the other, with green causeways between each, that an ancient art, long since become nature, had evidently designed and dug them, years, perhaps centuries, ago. So long dead were the old pond-makers that great trees grew now upon the causeways, and vast jungles of rush and water grasses choked the trickling overflows from one pond to

the other. Once, it was said, when the
earth of those parts had been rich in iron,
these ponds had driven great hammers, —
but long before the memory of the old-
est cottager they had rested from their
labours, and lived only the life of beauty
and silence. Where iron had once been
was now the wild rose, and the grim
wounds of the earth had been healed
by the kisses of five hundred springs.

About these ponds stole many a secret
path, veined with clumsy roots, shadowed
with the thick bush of many a cluster-
ing parasite, and echoing sometimes beneath from the hollowed shelter of coot
or water-rat. Lilies floated in circles
about the ponds, like the crowns of
sunken queens, and sometimes a bird
broke the silence with a frightened cry.

It was here that Beatrice and Wonder
would often take their morning walk, —
Wonder, though but a little girl of four,
having grown more and more of a com-

panion to her mother, since Antony's love for Silencieux.

A morning in August the two were walking hand in hand. Wonder was one of those little girls that seem to know all the meanings of life, while yet struggling with the alphabet of its unimportant words.

The soul of such a child is, of all things, the most mysterious. There was that in her face, as she clung on to her mother's hand, which seemed to say: " O mother, I understand it all, and far more ; if I might only talk to you in the language of heaven, — but my words are like my little legs, frail and uncertain of their footing, and, while I think all your strange grown-up thoughts, I can only talk of toys and dolls. Mother, father's blood as well as yours is in my veins, and so I understand you both. Poor little mother ! Poor little father ! "

Little Wonder looked these things, she

may indeed have thought them; but all she said was: " O mother, what was that?"

" That was a rabbit, dear. See, there is another! See his fluffy white tail ! "

And again: " O mother, what was that?"

" That was a water-hen, dear. She has a little house, a warm nest, close to the water among the bushes yonder, and she calls like that to let her little children know she's coming home with some dainty things for lunch. She means ' Hush! Hush! Don't be frightened. I'm coming just as fast as I can.' "

" Funny little mother! What pretty stories you tell me. But do the birds really talk — Oh, but look, little mother, there's Daddy — "

It was Antony, deep in some dream of Silencieux.

" Daddy! Daddy ! " cried the little girl.

He took her tenderly by the hand.

" Daddy, where have you been all this long time? You have brought me no flowers for ever so long."

" Flowers, little Wonder — they are nearly all gone away, gone to sleep till next year — But see, I will gather you something prettier than flowers."

And, hardly marking Beatrice, he led Wonder up and down among the winding underwood. Fungi of exquisite yellows and browns were popping up all about the wood. He gathered some of the most delicate, and put them into the fresh small hands.

" But, Daddy, I must n't eat them, must I ? "

" No, dear — they are too beautiful to eat. You must just look at them and love them, like flowers."

" But they are not flowers, Daddy. They don't smell like flowers. I would rather have flowers, Daddy."

" But there are no flowers till next

year. You must learn to love these too, little Wonder; they are more beautiful than flowers."

" Oh, no, Daddy, they are not — "

" Antony," said Beatrice, " how strange you are! Would you poison her? See, dear," (turning to Wonder) " Daddy is only teasing. Let us throw them away. They are nasty, nasty things. Promise me never to gather them, won't you, Wonder?"

" Yes, mother. I don't like them. They frighten me."

Antony turned into a by-path with a strange laugh, and was lost to them in the wood.

CHAPTER VII

THE LOVERS OF SILENCIEUX

SILENCIEUX often spoke to Antony now. Sometimes a sudden, startling word when he was writing late at night; sometimes long tender talks; once a terrible whisper. But all this time she never opened her eyes. The lashes still lay wet upon her cheeks, and when she spoke her lips seemed hardly to move, only to smile with a deeper meaning, an intenser life. Indeed, at these times, her face shone with so great a brightness that Antony's vision was dazzled, and to his gaze she seemed almost featureless as a star.

Once he had begged to see her eyes.

"You know not what you ask," she had answered. "When you see my eyes you will die. Some day, Antony, you shall see my eyes. But not yet. You have much to do for me yet. There is yet much love for you and me before the end."

"Have all died who saw your eyes, Silencieux?"

"Yes, all died."

"You have had many lovers, Silencieux. Many lovers, and far from here, and long ago."

"Yes, many lovers, long ago," echoed Silencieux.

"You have been very cruel, Silencieux."

"Yes, very cruel, but very kind. It is true men have died for me. I have been cruel, yes, but to die for me has seemed better than to live for any other. And some of my lovers I have never forsaken. When they have lost all in the world, they have had me. Lonely garrets have seemed richly furnished because of my face, and men with foodless lips have died blest because I was near them at the last. Sometimes I have kissed their lips and died with them, and the world has missed my face for a hundred unlovely years — for the world is only beautiful when I and my lovers are in it. Antony, you are one of my lovers, one of my dearest lovers; be great enough, be all mine, and perhaps I will die with you, Antony — and leave the world in darkness for your sake, another hundred years."

"Tell me of your lovers, Silencieux."

"Nearly three thousand years ago I loved a woman of Mitylene, very fair and made of fire. But she loved another more than I, and for his sake threw herself from a rock into the sea. As she fell, the rose we had made together fell from her bosom, and was torn to pieces by the sea. Fishermen gathered here and there a petal floating on the waters, — but what were they? — and the world has never known how wonderful was that rose of our love which she took with her into the depths of the sea."

"You are faithful, Silencieux; you love her still."

"Yes, I love her still."

"And with whom did love come next, Silencieux?"

"Oh, I loved many those years, for the loss of a great love sends us vainly from hand to hand of many lesser loves, to ease a little the great ache; and at that time the world seemed full of my lovers. I have forgotten none of them. They pass before me, a fair frieze of unforgotten faces; but most I loved a Roman poet, because, perhaps, he loved so well the memory of her I had loved, and knew so skilfully to make bloom again among his own red roses those petals of passionate ivory which the fishermen of Lesbos had recovered from the sea."

"Tell me of your lovers, Silencieux," said Antony again.

"Hundreds of years after, I loved in Florence a young poet with a face of silver. His soul was given to a little red-cheeked girl. She died, and then I took him to my bosom, and loved him on through the years, till his face had grown iron with many sorrows. Now at last, his baby-girl by his side, he sits in heaven, with a face of gold. In Paris," she went on, " have I been wonderfully beloved, and in northern lands near the pole — "

" But—England?" said Antony. "Tell me of your English lovers."

" Best of them I love two : one a laughing giant who loved me three hundred years ago, and the other a little London boy with large eyes of velvet, who mid all the gloom of your great city saw and loved my face, as none had seen and loved it since she of Mitylene. I found the giant sitting by a country stream, holding a daffodil in his mighty hands and whistling to the birds. He took and wore me like a flower. I was to him as a nightingale that sang from his sleeve, for he loved so much

4

besides. Yet me he loved best, as those who can read his secret poems understand. But my little London boy loved me only. For him the world held nothing but my face, and it was of his great love for me that he died."

"But these were all poets," said Antony.

"Yes, poets are the greatest of all lovers. Though all who since the world began have been the makers of beautiful things have loved me, I love my poets best. Sweeter than marble or many colours to my eyes is the sound of a poet singing in my ears —"

"For whom, Silencieux, did you step down into the sad waters of the Seine?"

"It was a young poet of Paris, beloved of many women, a drunkard of strange dreams. He too died because he loved me, and when he died there was none left whose voice seemed sweet after his. So I died with him. I died with him," she re-

peated, " to come to life again with you.
Many lips have been pressed to mine,
Antony, since the cold sleep of the Seine
fell over me, but none were warm and
wild like yours. I loved my sleep while
the others kissed me, but with the touch
of your lips the dreams of life began to
stir within me again. O Antony, be great
enough, be all mine, that we may fulfil
our dream; and perhaps, Antony, I will
die with you — and leave the world in
darkness for your sake, another hundred
years."

Exalted above the earth with the joy of
Silencieux's words, Antony pressed his
lips to hers in an ecstasy, and vowed his
life and all within it inviolably to her.

CHAPTER VIII

A STRANGE KISS FOR SILENCIEUX

ONE hot August afternoon Antony took Silencieux with him to a bramble-covered corner of the dark moor which bounded his little wood. A ruined bank soaked with sunshine, a haunt of lizards, a cata-comb of little lives that creep and run and whisper, made their seat.

Silencieux's face, out there under the open sky and in the full blaze of the sun, at once lost and gained in reality ; gained by force of a contrast which accentuated while it limited her, lost by opposition to the great faces of earth and sky. Her life, so concentrated, so self-absorbed, seemed more of an essence, potently distilled, compared with this abounding ichor of existence, that audibly sang in brimming circulation through the veins of this care-lessly immortal earth.

For some moments of self-conscious thought she shrank into a symbol, — a symbol of but one of the elements of the mighty world. Yet to this element did not all the others, more brutal in force, more extended in space, conspire?

So in some hours will the most mortal maid of warmest flesh and blood become an abstraction to her lover — sometimes shrink to the significance of one more flower, and sometimes expand to the signifi-cance of a microcosm, a firmament in mystical miniature.

Thus in like manner for Antony did Silencieux alternate between reality and dream that afternoon, though all the time he knew that, however now and again the daylight seemed to create an illusion of her remoteness, she was still his, and he of all men her chosen lover.

Suddenly as they sat there together,

silent and immovable, Antony caught the peer of two bright little eyes fixed on the white face of Silencieux. A tiny wedge-shaped head, with dashes of white across the brows, reared itself out of a crevice in the bank. A forked tongue came and went like black lightning through its eager little lips, and a handsomely marked adder began to glide, like molten metal, along the bank to Silencieux. The brilliant whiteness of the image had fascinated the little creature.

Antony kept very still. Darting its head from side to side, venomously alert against the smallest sound, the adder reached Silencieux. Then to Antony's delight it coiled itself round the white throat, still restlessly moving its head wonderingly beneath the chin. With a grace to which all movement from the beginning of time seemed to have led up, it clasped Silencieux's neck and softly reared its lips to hers. Its black tongue darted to and fro along that strange smile.

"He has kissed her!" Antony exclaimed, and in an instant the adder was nothing more than a terrified rustle in the brushwood.

He took Silencieux into his hands. There was poison on her lips. For another moment his fancy made him self-conscious, and turned Silencieux again into a symbol, — though it was but for a moment.

" There is always poison on the lips of Art," he said to himself.

CHAPTER IX

THE WONDERFUL WEEK

As Antony and Silencieux became more and more to each other, poor Beatrice, though she had been the first occasion of their love, and little as she now demanded, seldom as Antony spoke to her, seldom as he smiled upon her, distant as were the lonely walks she took, infrequent as was her sad footfall in the little wood, — poor Beatrice, though indeed, so far from active intrusion upon their loves, and as if only by her breathing with them the heavy air of that green unwholesome valley, was becoming an irksome presence of the imagination. They longed to be somewhere together where Beatrice had never been, where her sad face could not follow them; and one night Silencieux whispered to Antony:—

"Take me to the sea, Antony — to some lonely sea."

"To-morrow I will take you," said Antony, "where the loneliest land meets the loneliest sea."

On the morrow evening the High Muses had once more made Antony late for dinner. One hour, and two hours, went by, and then Beatrice, in alarm, took the lantern and courageously braved the blackness of the wood.

The châlet was in darkness, and the door was locked, but through the uncurtained glass of the window, she was able to irradiate the emptiness of its interior. Antony was not there.

But she noticed, with a shudder, that the space usually filled by the Image was vacant. Then she understood, and with a hopeless sigh went down the wood again.

Already Antony and Silencieux had

found the place where the loneliest land meets the loneliest sea.   Side by side they were sitting on a moonlit margin of the world, and Antony was singing low to the murmur of the waves : —

Hopeless of hope, past desire even of thee,
     There is one place I long for,
       A desolate place
     That I sing all my songs for,
     A desolate place for a desolate face,
Where the loneliest land meets the loneliest sea.

Green waves and green grasses — and nought else is
     nigh,
     But a shadow that beckons ;
       A desolate face,
     And a shadow that beckons
     The desolate face to the desolate place
Where the loneliest sea meets the loneliest sky.

Wide sea and wide heaven, and all else afar,
     But a spirit is singing,
       A desolate soul
     That is joyfully winging —
     A desolate soul — to that desolate goal
Where the loneliest wave meets the loneliest star.

" It is not good," said Silencieux.

" I know," answered Antony.

" Throw it into the sea."

" It is not worthy of the sea."

" Burn it."

" Fire is too august."

" Throw it to the winds."

" They are too busy."

" Bury it."

" It would make barren a whole meadow."

" Forget it."

" I will — And you ? "

" I will."

And Antony and Silencieux laughed softly together by the sea.

Many days Antony and Silencieux stayed together by the sea. They loved it together in all its changes, in sun and rain, in wild wind and dreamy calm ; at morning when it shone like a spirit, at evening when it flickered like a ghost, at noon when it lay asleep curled up like

a woman in the arms of the land.   Sometimes at evening they sat in the little fish-
ing harbour, watching the incoming boats,
till the sky grew sad with rigging and old
men's faces.

Then at last Silencieux said : " I am
weary of the sea.   Let us go to the town
— to the lights and the sad cries of the
human waves."

So they went to the town and found a
room high up, where they sat at the window and watched the human lights, and
listened to the human music.

Never had it been so wonderful to be
together.

For a week Antony lived in heaven.
Never had Silencieux been so kind, so
close to him.

" Let us be little children," he said.
" Let us do anything that comes into our
heads."

So they ran in and out among pleasures
together, joined strange dances and sang

strange songs. They clapped their hands
to jugglers and acrobats, and animals tortured into talent. And sometimes, as the
gaudy theatre resounded about them, they
looked so still at each other that all the
rest faded away, and they were left alone
with each other's eyes and great thoughts
of God.

"I love you, Silencieux."

"I love you, Antony."

"You will never leave me lonely in my
dream, Silencieux?"

"Never, Antony."

Oh, how tender sometimes was Silencieux!

Several nights they had the whim that
Silencieux should masquerade in the ward-
robe of her past.

"To-night, you shall go clothed as
when you loved that woman in Mitylene,"
Antony would say.

Or: "To-night you shall be a little
shepherd-boy, with a leopard-skin across

your shoulder and mountain berries in your hair."

Or again : " To-night you shall be Pierrot — mourning for his Columbine."

Ah ! how divine was Silencieux in all her disguises ! — a divine child. Oh, how tender those nights was Silencieux !

Antony sat and watched her face in awe and wonder. Surely it was the noblest face that had ever been seen in the world.

" Is it true that that noble face is mine ? " he would ask ; " I cannot believe it."

" Kiss it," said Silencieux gaily, " and see."

Then on a sudden, what was this change in Silencieux !   So cold, so silent, so cruel, had she grown.

" Silencieux," Antony called to her. " Silencieux," he pleaded.

But she never spoke.

" O Silencieux, speak ! I cannot bear it."

Then her lips moved. " Shall I speak ? " she said, with a cruel smile.

" Yes," he besought her again.

" I shall love you no more in this world. The lights are gone out, the magic faded."

" Silencieux ! "

But she spoke no more, and, with those lonely words in his ears, Antony came out of his dream and heard the rain falling miserably through the wood.

CHAPTER X

SILENCIEUX WHISPERS

So Antony first knew how cruel could be
Silencieux to those who loved her. Her
sudden silences he had grown to understand, even to love. Always they had
been broken again by some wonderful
word, which he had known would come
sooner or later. All great natures are full
of silence. Silence is the soil of all passion.
But now it was not silence that was between them, but terrible speech. As with
a knife she had stabbed their love right in
its heart. Yet Antony knew that his love
could never die, but only suffer.

During these days he half turned to
Beatrice. How kind was her simple earth-
warm affection, after the star-cold trans-
cendentalism in which he had been living!

How full of comfort was her unselfish humanity, after the pitiless egoism of the divine !

And yet, while it momentarily soothed him, he realised, with a heart sad for Beatrice as for himself, that it could never satisfy him again. For days he left Silencieux alone in the wood, and Beatrice's face brightened with their renewed companionship ; but all the time he seemed to hear Silencieux calling him, and he knew that he would have to go back.

One night, almost happy again, as he lay by the side of Beatrice, who was sleeping deeply, he rose stealthily, and looked out into the wood.

The moonlight fell through it mysteriously, as on that night when he had stolen up there to meet Silencieux — " at the rising of the moon." He could hesitate no longer. Leaving Beatrice asleep, he was soon making his way once more through the moonlit trees.

5

The little châlet looked very still and solemn, like a temple of Chaldean mysteries, and an unwonted chill of fear passed through Antony as he stood in the circle of moonlight outside.   His spirit seemed aware of some dread menace to the future in that moment, and a voice was crying within him to go back.

But the longing that had brought him so far was too strong for such undefined warnings.   Once more he turned the key in the lock, and looked on Silencieux once more.

The moonlight fell over her face like a veil of silver, and on her eyelashes was a glitter of tears.

Her face was alive again, alive too with a softness of womanhood he had never seen before.

"Forgive me, Antony," she said.   "I loved you all the time."

What else need Silencieux say !

"But it was so strange," said Antony

after a while, " so strange. I could have borne the pain, if only I could have understood."

"Shall I tell you the reason, Antony ? "

" Yes."

" It was because I saw in your eyes a thought of Beatrice. For a moment your thoughts had forsaken me and gone to pity Beatrice. I saw it in your eyes."

" Poor Beatrice ! " said Antony. " It is little indeed I give her. Could you not spare her so little, Silencieux ? "

" I can spare her nothing. You must be all mine, Antony — your every thought and hope and dream. So long as there is another woman in the world for you except me, I cannot be yours in the depths of my being, nor you mine. There must always be something withheld. It will never be perfect, until — "

" Until when ? "

" Until, Antony," — and Silencieux lowered her voice to an awful whisper,

— "until you have made for me the human sacrifice."

" The human sacrifice ! "

" Yes, Antony, — all my lovers have done that for me. They were not really mine till then. Some have brought me many such offerings. Antony, when will you bring me the human sacrifice ? "

" O Silencieux ! "

Antony's heart chilled with terror at Silencieux's words. It was against this that the voices had warned him as he came up the wood. O that he had never seen Silencieux more, never heard her poisonous voice again !

As one fleeing before the shadow of uncommitted sin that gains upon him at each stride, Antony fled from the place, and sought the moors. The moon was near its setting, and soon the dawn would throw open the eastern doors of the sky. He walked on and on, waiting, praying for, stifling for the light; and, at last, with a freshening of the air, and faint sounds of returning consciousness from distant farms, it came.

High over a lake of ethereal silver welling up out of space, hung the morning star, shining as though its heart would break, bright as a tear that must slip down the face of heaven and fall amid the grass.

As Antony looked up at it, his soul escaped from its prison of dark thought, and such an exaltation had come with the quickening light, that it seemed as though the body, with little more than pure aspiration to wing it, might follow the soul's flight to that crystal sphere.

In that moment, Antony knew that the love in the soul of man is mated only with the infinite universe. In no marriage less than that shall it find lasting fulfilment of itself. No single face, however beautiful, no single human soul, however vast, can absorb it. Silencieux,

Beatrice, Wonder, himself, all faded away, in a trance-like sense of a stupendous passion, an august possession. He felt that within him which rose up gigantic from the earth, and towered into eyries of space, from whence that morning star seemed like a dewdrop glittering low down upon the earth.

It was the god in him that knew itself for one brief space, a moment's awakening in the sleep of fact.

Could a god so great, so awakened, be again the slave of one earthly face?

Yes, the greater the god, the greater the slave; and so it was that, falling plumb down from that skyey exaltation, human again with the weakness that follows divine moments, Antony returned from the morning star to Silencieux.

Her face was bathed in the delicate early sunlight and looked very pure and gentle, and he kissed her.

Surely those terrible words had been an

illusion of the dark hours. Silencieux had never said them. He kissed her again.

"I love you, Silencieux," he said. And then she spoke.

"If you love me, Antony," she said, "if you love me — "

"O what, Silencieux?" he cried, his heart growing cold once more.

"Come nearer, Antony. Put your ear to my lips — Antony, if you love me — the human sacrifice."

"O God," he cried, "here in the sun-light — It is true — "

And, a man with the doom of his nature heavy upon him, he once more went out into the wood.

CHAPTER XI

WONDER IN THE WOOD

A FEW days after this, little Wonder, playing about the garden, had slipped away from her nurse, and, pleased in her little soul at her cleverness, had found her way up to her father's châlet. Antony was sitting at his desk, writing, with his door open.

" Daddy," suddenly came a little voice from the bottom of the staircase, " Daddy, where are you? "

Antony rose and went to the door.

" Come in, little Wonder. Well, it is a clever girl to come all the way up the wood by herself."

" Yes, Daddy," said the self-possessed little girl, as she toddled into the châlet and looked round wonderingly at the books and pictures. Then presently :

" Daddy, what do you do all day in the wood ? "

" I make beautiful things."

" Show me some."

Antony showed her a page of his beautiful manuscript.

" Why, those are only words, silly Daddy ! "

" But words, little Wonder, are the most beautiful things in the world. Listen — " and he took the child on his knee. " Listen : —

> In Xanadu did Kubla Khan
> A stately pleasure-dome decree :
> Where Alph, the sacred river, ran
> Through caverns measureless to man
> Down to a sunless sea.

The child had inherited a love of beautiful sound, and, though she understood nothing of the meaning, the music charmed her, and she nestled close to her father, with wide eyes.

"Say some more, Daddy."

The sobbing cadences of the greatest of Irish songs came to Antony's mind, and he crooned a verse or two at random:

> All day long, in unrest,
> To and fro, do I move.
> The very soul within my breast
> Is wasted for you, love !
> The heart in my bosom faints
> To think of you, my queen,
> My life of life, my saint of saints,
>   My dark Rosaleen!
>   My own Rosaleen !
> To hear your sweet and sad complaints,
> My life, my love, my saint of saints,
>   My dark Rosaleen ! . . . .
>
> Over dews, over sands,
> Will I fly for your weal :
> Your holy delicate white hands
> Shall girdle me with steel.
> At home in your emerald bowers,
> From morning's dawn till e'en,

You 'll pray for me, my flower of flowers,
     My dark Rosaleen !
     My fond Rosaleen !
You 'll think of me thro' daylight hours,
My virgin flower, my flower of flowers,
     My dark Rosaleen !

I could scale the blue air,
I could plough the high hills,
Oh, I could kneel all night in prayer
     To heal your many ills !
And one beamy smile from you
Would float like light between
My toils and me, my own, my true,
     My dark Rosaleen !
     My fond Rosaleen !
Would give me life and soul anew,
A second life, a soul anew,
     My dark Rosaleen !

Wonder, child-like, wearied with the length of the verses, and suddenly the white face of Silencieux caught her eye.

" Who is that lady, Daddy ? "

"That is Silencieux."

" What a pretty name ! Is she a kind lady, Daddy ?"

" Sometimes."

" She is very beautiful. She is like little mother. But her face is so white. She makes me frightened. Hold me, Daddy — " and she crouched in his arms.

"You must n't be frightened of her, Wonder. She loves little girls. See how she is smiling at you. She wants to be friends with you. She wants you to kiss her, little Wonder."

" Oh, no! no!" almost screamed the little girl.

But suddenly a cruel whim to insist came over the father, and, half-coaxingly and half-forcibly, he held her up to the image, stroking its white cheek to reassure her.

" See, how kind she is, little Wonder! See how she smiles — how she loves you. She loves little girls, and she never sees any up here in the lonely wood. It will make her so happy. Kiss her, little Wonder!"

Reluctantly the child obeyed, and with a shudder she said : —

" Oh, how cold her lips are, Daddy ! "

" But were they not sweet, little Wonder ? "

" No, Daddy, they tasted of dust."

And as Antony had lifted her up, he had said in his heart : " Silencieux, I bring you my little child."

CHAPTER XII

AUTUMN IN THE VALLEY

AUTUMN in the valley was autumn, melancholy and sinister, as you find her only in such low-lying immemorial drifting places of leaves, and oozy sinks of dank water. For the moors autumn is the spring come back in purple, and in golden woods and many another place where the year dies happily, she smiles like a widow so young and fair that one thinks rather of life than death in her presence.

But in the valley Autumn was a fearsome hag, a little crazy, two-double, gathering sticks in a scarlet cloak. When she turned her wicked old eyes upon you, the life died within you, and wherever you walked she was always somewhere

in the bushes muttering evil spells. All
the year round under the green cloud
of summer, you might meet Autumn
creeping somewhere in the valley, like
foul mists that creep from pool to
pool; for here all the year was decay
to feed upon and dead leaves for her to
sleep on. Always the year round in the
valley, if you listened close, you would
hear something sighing, something dying.
To the happiest walking there would
come strange sinkings of the heart, un-
accountable premonitions of overhang-
ing doom. There the least superstitious
would start at the sight of a toad, and
come upon three magpies at once not without fear. Over all was a breath of im-
minent disaster, a look of sorrow from
which there was no escape. It was not
many yards away from a merry high-
road, but once in the shade of its lanes, it
seemed as though you had been shut
away from the world of living men.

Black slopes of pine and melancholy bars of sunset walled you in, as in some funeral hall of judgment.

Alas! Beatrice's was not the happiest of hearts, and all day long this autumn, as the mornings came later and darker and the evenings earlier, always voices in the valley, voices of low-hanging mist and dripping rain, kept saying: " Death is coming! Death is coming!"

Tapped at the windows, ticking and crying in the rooms, was the same message; till, in a terror of the walls, she would flee into the wider prison of the woods, and oppressed by them in turn, would escape with a beating heart into the honest daylight of the high-road. So one flies from a haunted house, or comes out of an evil dream.

Sometimes it seemed as if the white face of Silencieux looked out from the woodside, and mocked her with the same cry: " Death is coming! Death is coming!"

Silencieux! Ah, how happy they had been before the coming of Silencieux! How frail is our happiness, how suddenly it can die! One moment it seems built for eternity, marble-based and glittering with towers, — the next, where it stood is lonely grass and dew, not a stone left. Ah, yes, how happy they had been; and then Antony by a heartless chance had seen Silencieux, and in an instant their happiness had been at an end for ever. Only a glance of the eyes and love is born, only a glance of the eyes, and alas! love must die.

A glance of the eyes and all the old kindness is gone, a glance of the eyes, and from the face you love the look you seek has died out for everlasting.

"O Antony! Antony!" moaned Beatrice, as she wandered alone in those dank autumn lanes, "if you would only come back to me for one short day, come back with the old look on your face, be to me

6

for a little while as you once were, I think
I could gladly die — "

Die ! A tattered flower caught her
glance, shaking chilly in the damp wind,
and once more she heard the whisper,
" Death is coming ! "

Near where she walked, stood, in the
midst of a small meadow overgrown with
nettles, the blackened ruin of a cottage
long since destroyed by fire. On the edge
of the little sandy lane, perilously near the
feet of the passer-by, was its forgotten
well, the mouth choked with weeds and
briers.

In her absorption Beatrice had almost
walked into it. Now she parted the
bushes and looked down. A stone fell
as she looked, making a sepulchral echo.
What a place to hide one's sorrow in !
No one would think of looking there.
Antony might think she had gone away,
or he might drag the three black ponds,
but here it was unlikely any one would

come. And in a little while — a very little while — Antony would forget, or sometimes make himself happy with his unhappiness.

Ah! but Wonder! No, if Antony needed her no more, Wonder did. She must stay for Wonder's sake. And perhaps, who could say, Antony might yet need her, might come to her some day and say "Beatrice," with the old voice. To be really necessary to Antony again, if only for one little hour, — yes! she could wait and suffer for that.

CHAPTER XIII

THE HUMAN SACRIFICE

THE valley was an ill place even for the body, a lair of rheums and agues ; and disembodied fevers waited in wells for the sunk pail.   For the valley was very beautiful, beautiful with that green beauty that only comes of damp and decay.

Late one October night, Antony, alone with Silencieux, as was now again his custom, was surprised to hear footsteps coming hastily up the wood, and even more surprised at the sudden unusual appearance of Beatrice.

"I am sorry to disturb you, Antony," she said, noting with a pang how the lamp had been arranged to throw a vivid light upon Silencieux, " but I want you to come down and look at Wonder. I 'm afraid she is ill."

"Wonder, ill !" exclaimed Antony, rising with a start, " I will come at once ; " and they went together.

Wonder was lying in her bed, with flushed cheeks and bright yet heavy eyes.

"Wonder, my little Wonder," said Antony caressingly, as he bent over her. " Does little Wonder feel ill ? "

"Yes, Daddy. I feel so sick, Daddy."

"Never mind ; she will be better to-morrow." But he had noticed how burning hot were her hands, and how dry were her fresh little lips.

" I must go for the doctor at once," he said to his wife, when they were outside the room. The father, so long asleep, had sprung awake at the first hint of danger to the little child that in his neglectful way he loved deeply all the time ; and, in spite of the danger to Wonder, a faint joy stirred in Beatrice's heart to see him thus humanly aroused once more.

" Kiss me, Beatrice," he said, as he set out upon his errand. " Don't be anxious, it will be all right."   It was the first time he had kissed his wife for many days.

The doctor's was some three miles away across the moor.   It was a bright starlit night, and Antony, who knew the moor well, had no difficulty in making his way at a good pace along the mossy tracks. Presently he gave a little cry of pain and stood still.

" O God," he cried, " it cannot be that. Oh, it cannot."

At that moment for the first time a dreadful thought had crossed his mind. Suddenly a memory of that afternoon when he had bade Wonder kiss Silencieux flashed upon him; and once more he heard himself saying : " Silencieux, I bring you my little child."

But he had never meant it so.   It had

all been a mad fancy. What was Silencieux herself but a wilful, selfish dream?
He saw it all now. How could a lifeless
image have power over the life of his
child?

And yet again, was Silencieux a lifeless
image? And still again, if she were an
image, was it not always to an image that
humanity from the beginning had been
sacrificed? Yes; perhaps if Silencieux
were only an image there was all the more
reason to fear her.

When he returned he would go to
Silencieux, go on his knees and beg for
the life of his child. Silencieux had been
cruel, but she could hardly be so cruel as
that.

He drove back across the moor by the
doctor's side.

" I have always thought you unwise
to live in that valley," said the doctor.
" It's pretty, but like most pretty places,
it's unhealthy. Nature can seldom be

good and beautiful at the same time." The doctor was somewhat of a philosopher.

"Your little girl needs the hills. In fact you all do. Your wife is n't half the woman she was since you took her into the valley. You don't look any better for it, either. No, sir, believe me, beauty's all very well, but it's not good to live with — And, by the way, have you had your well looked at lately? That valley is just a beautiful sewer for the drainage of the hills; a very market-town for all the germs and bacilli of the district."

And the doctor laughed, as, curiously enough, people always do at jests about bacilli.

But when he looked at Wonder, he took a more serious view of bacilli.

"You must have your well looked to at once," he said. "Your little girl is very ill. She must be kept very quiet, and on no account excited."

Beatrice and Antony took it in turns to

watch by Wonder's bed that night, and once while Beatrice was watching, Antony found time to steal up the wood with his prayer to Silencieux.

Never had she looked more mask-like, more lifeless.

" Silencieux," he cried, " I wickedly brought you my little child. O give her back to me again ! I cannot bear it. I cannot give her to you, Silencieux. Take me, if you will. I will gladly die for you. But spare her. O give her back to me, Silencieux ! "

But the image was impassive and made no sign.

" Silencieux," he implored, " speak, for I know you hear me. Are you a devil, Silencieux ; a devil I have worshipped all this time ? God help me ! Have you no pity, — what is her little flower-life to you ? Why should you snatch it out of the sun — "

But Silencieux made no sign.

Then Antony grew angry in his remorse : " I hate you, Silencieux. Never
will I look on your face again. You are
an evil dream that has stolen from me the
truth of life. I have broken a true heart
that loved me, that would have died for
me — for your sake ; just to watch your
loveless beauty, to hear the cold music
of your voice. You are like the moon
that turns men mad, a hollow shell of
silver drawing all your light from the sun
of life, a silver shadow of the golden sun."

But prayer and reproach were alike in
vain. Silencieux remained unheeding, and
Antony returned to watch by Beatrice's
side, with a heart that had now no hope,
and a soul weighed down with the sense
of irrevocable sin. There lay the little
life he had murdered, delivered up to the
Moloch of Art. No sorrow, no agonies,
were now of any avail for ever. Little
Wonder would surely die, and all the old
lost opportunities of loving her could

never return.   He had loved the shadow.
This was a part of the price.

Day after day the cruel fever consumed
Wonder as fire consumes a flower.   Her
tiny face seemed too small for the visita-
tion of such suffering as burned and ham-
mered behind the high white brow, and
yellowed and drew tight the skin upon the
cheeks.   She had so recently known the
strange pain of being born.   Already, for
so little of life, she was to endure the pain
of death.

Day after day, hour after hour, Antony
hung over her bed, with a devotion and
an unconsciousness of fatigue that made
Beatrice look at him with astonishment,
and sometimes even for a moment forget
Wonder in the joy with which she saw
him transfigured by simple human love.
Now, when it was too late, he had become
a father indeed.   And it brought some
case to his fiercely tortured heart to notice
that it was his ministrations that the dying

child seemed to welcome most. For the most part she lay in a semi-conscious state, heeding nothing, and only moaning now and again, a sad little moan, like an injured bird. She seemed to say she was so little a thing to suffer so. Once, however, when Antony had just placed some fresh ice around her head, she opened her eyes and said, " Dear little Daddy," and the light on Antony's face — poor victim of perverse instincts that too often drew his really fine nature awry — was sanctifying to see.

As terrible was the look of torture that came over his face, one night near the end, when Wonder in a sudden nightmare of delirium had seized his hand and cried : —

" O Daddy, the white lady ! See her there at the end of the bed. She is smiling, Daddy — " Then lower, " You will not make me kiss her any more, will you, Daddy ? " —

Beatrice had gone to snatch an hour or two's sleep, so she never heard this, and it was no mere cowardly consolation for Antony to think afterwards that no one but he and his little child had known of that fatal afternoon in the wood. The dead understand all, — yes, even the dead we have murdered. But the living can never be told a secret such as that which Antony and his little daughter, whose soul was really grown up, though she spoke still in baby language, shared immortally between them.

When Beatrice returned to the room Wonder was sleeping peacefully again, but at the chill hour when watchers blow out the night-lights, and a dreary greyness comes like a fog through the curtains, Antony and Beatrice fell into each other's arms in anguish, for Wonder was dead.

CHAPTER XIV

A SONG OF THE LITTLE DEAD

THEY carried little Wonder to a green churchyard, a place of kind old trees and tender country bells. There were few birds to welcome her in the grim November morning, but the grasses stole close and whispered that very soon the thrush and the nightingale would be coming, that the violets were already on their way, and that when May was there she should lie all day in a bed of perfume.

For very dear to Nature's heart are the Little Dead. The great dead lie imprisoned in escutcheoned vaults, but for the little dead Nature spreads out soft small graves, all snowdrops and dewdrops, where day-long they can feel the earth rocking them as in a cradle, and at night hear the hushed singing of the stars.

Yes, Earth loves nothing so much as her little graves. There the tiny bodies, like unexhausted censers, pour out all the stored sweetness they had no time to use above the ground, turning the earth they lie in to precious spices. There the roots of the old yew trees feel about tenderly for the little unguided hands, and sometimes at nightfall the rain bends over them weeping like an inconsolable mother.

It is on the little graves that the sun first rises at morn, and it is there at evening that the moon lays softly her first silver flowers.

There the wren will sometimes bring her sky-blue eggs for a gift, and the summer wind come sowing seeds of magic to take the fancy of the little one beneath. Sometimes it shakes the hyacinths like a rattle of silver, and spreads the turf above with a litter of coloured toys.

Here the butterflies are born with the first warm breath of the spring. All the winter they lie hidden in the crevices of the stone, in the carving of little names, and with the first spring day they stand delicately and dry their yellow wings on the little graves. There are the honey-combs of friendly bees, and the shelters of many a timid earth-born speck of life no bigger than a dewdrop, mysteriously small. Radiant pin-points of existence have their palaces on the broad blades of the grasses, and in the cellars at their roots works many a humble little slave of the mighty elements.

Yes, the emperors and the ants of Nature's vast economy alike love to be kind to the little graves.

CHAPTER XV

SILENCIEUX ALONE IN THE WOOD.

BEATRICE's grief for Wonder was such as only a mother can know. She had but one consolation, — the kind sad eyes of Antony. She had lost Wonder, but Antony had come back again. Wonder was not so dead as Antony had seemed a month ago.

When they had left Wonder and were back in the house which was now twice desolate, Antony took Beatrice's hands very tenderly and said : —

" I have been very wrong all these months. For a shadow I have missed the lovely reality of a little child — and for a shadow, my own faithful wife, I have all this time done you cruel wrong. But my

7

eyes are open now, I have come out of the evil dream that bound me — and never shall I enter it again. Let us go from here. Let us leave this valley and never come back to it any more."

So it was arranged that they should winter far away, returning only to the valley for a few short days in the spring, and then leave it for ever. They had no heart now for more than just to fly from that haunted place, and before night fell in the valley they were already far away.

In vain Silencieux listened for the sound of her lover's step in the wood, for he had vowed that he would never look upon her face again.

CHAPTER XVI

THE FIRST TALK ON THE HILLS

ANTONY took Beatrice to the high hills where all the year long the sun and the snow shine together. He was afraid of the sea, for the sea was Silencieux's for ever. In its depths lay a magic harp which filled all its waves with music — music lovely and accursed, the voice of Silencieux. That he must never hear again. He would pile the hills against his ears. Inland and upland, he and Beatrice should go, ever closer to the kind heart of the land, ever nearer to the forgetful silences of the sky, till huge walls of space were between them and that harp of the sea. Nor in the whisper of leaves nor in the gloom of forests should the thought of Silencieux beset them. The earth that held least of her — to that earth they would go ;. the earth that rose nearest to heaven.

Beauty indeed should be theirs — the Beauty of Nature and Love ; no more the vampire's beauty of Art.

It was strange to each how their souls lightened as the valleys of the world folded away behind them, and the simple slopes mounted in their path. In that pure unladen air which so exhilarated their very bodies, there seemed some mysterious property of exhilaration for the soul also. One might have dreamed that just to breathe on those heights all one's days would be to grow holy by the more cleansing power of the air. With such bright currents ever running through the brain, surely one's thoughts would circle there white as stones at the bottom of a spring.

" O Antony," said Beatrice, " why were we so long in finding the hills ? "

" We found them once before, Beatrice
— do you remember ? "

" Yes ! You have not forgotten ? "
said Beatrice, with the ray of a lost happiness in her eyes — lost, and yet could it be
dawning again ? There was a morning
star in Antony's face.

" And then," said Antony, " we went
into the valley — the Valley of Beauty and
Death."

Beatrice pressed his hand and looked
all her love at him for comfort. He
knew how precious was such a forgiveness,
the forgiveness of a mother heart broken
for the child, which he, directly or indirectly, had sacrificed, — directly as he
and Wonder alone knew, indirectly by
taking them with him into the Valley of
Beauty.

" Ah, Beatrice, your love is almost
greater than I can bear. I am not worthy
of it. I never shall be worthy. There
is something in the love of a woman like

you to which the best man is unequal. We can love — and greatly — but it is not the same."

"We went into the valley," he cried, "and I lost you your little Wonder — "

"*Our* little Wonder," gently corrected Beatrice. "We found her together, and we lost her together. Perhaps some day we shall find her together again — "

"And do you know, Antony," Beatrice continued, "I sometimes wonder if her little soul was not sent and so taken away all as part of a mission to us, which in its turn is a part of the working out of her own destiny. For life is very mysterious, Antony — "

"Alas! I had forgotten life," answered Antony with a sigh.

"Yes, dear," Beatrice went on, pursuing her thought. "I have dared to hope that perhaps Wonder, as she was the symbol of our coming together, was taken away just at this time because we were being drawn apart. Perhaps it was to save our love that little Wonder died — "

Antony looked at Beatrice, half as one looks at a child, and half as one might look at an angel.

" Beatrice," he said tenderly, " you believe in God."

" All women believe in God," answered Beatrice.

" Yes," said Antony musingly, and with no thought of irony, " it is that which makes you women."

CHAPTER XVII

ANTONY ALONE ON THE HILLS

But although Beatrice might forgive Antony, from himself came no forgiveness. He hid his remorse from her, sparing the mother-wound in her heart — but always when he was walking alone he kept saying to himself: " I have lost our little Wonder. I killed our little Wonder."

One day he climbed up the highest hill within reach, and there leaned into the enormous silence, that he might cry it aloud for God to hear —

God ! — poor little Beatrice, what God was there to hear ! To look at Beatrice one might indeed believe in God — and yet was it not Beatrice who had

made God in her own image? Was
not God created of all pure overflows
of the human soul, the kind light of
human eyes that not all the suffering
of the world can exhaust, the idealism of
the human spirit that not all the infamies
of natural law can dismay?

Nevertheless, Antony confessed himself
to God upon the hills, not indeed as one
seeking pardon, but punishment.

Yet Heaven's benign untroubled blue
carried no cloud upon its face, because one
breaking human heart had thus breathed
into it its unholy secret. Around that
whole enormous circle such cries and such
confessions were being poured like nox-
ious vapours, from a thousand cities; but
that incorruptible ether remained unsullied
as on the first morning, the black smoke
of it all lost in the optimism of God.

On some days he would live over again
the scene with Wonder in the wood with
unbearable vividness.

"Why, those are only words, silly Daddy!" — How many times a day did he not hear that quaint little voice making, with a child's profundity, that tremendous criticism upon literature.

He had silenced her with the music of words, as he had silenced his own heart and soul with the same music, but they were still only words none the less. Ah! if she were only here to-day, he would bring her something more beautiful than words — or toadstools.

He shuddered as he thought of the loathsome form his decaying fancy had taken, that morning by the Three Black Ponds. He had filled the small outstretched hands with Nature's filth and poison. She had asked for flowers, he had brought her toadstools. Oh, the shame, the crime, the anguish!

But worst of all was to hear himself saying in the silence of his soul, over and over again without any power to still it, as one is forced sometimes to hear the beating of one's heart: " Silencieux, I bring you my little child."

There were times he heard this so plainly when he was with Beatrice that he had to leave her and walk for hours alone. Only unseen among the hills dare he give vent to the mad despair with which that memory tore him.

Yes, for words — " only words " — he had sacrificed that wonderful living thing, a child. For words he had missed that magical intercourse, the intercourse with the mind of a child. How often had she come to him for a story, and he had been dull and preoccupied — with words ; how often asked him to take her a walk up the lane, but he had been too busy — with words !

O God, if only she might come and ask again. Now when she was so far away his fancy teemed with stories. Every roadside flower had its fairy-tale which cried, "Tell me to little Wonder"—and once he tried to make believe to himself that Wonder was holding his hand, and looking up into his face with her big grave eyes, as he told some child's nonsense to the eternal hills. He broke off—half in anger with himself. Was he changing one illusion for another?

"Fool, no one hears you," and he threw himself face down in the grass and sobbed.

But a gentle hand was laid upon his shoulder and Beatrice's voice said,—

"I heard you, Antony—and loved you for it."

So Antony had found the heart of a father when no longer he had a child.

CHAPTER XVIII

THE SECOND TALK ON THE HILLS

" But to think," said Antony presently, in answer to Beatrice's soothing hand, "to think that I might have lived with a child — and I chose instead to live with words. In all the mysterious ways of man, is there anything quite so mysterious as that? Poor dream-led fool, poor lover of coloured shadows!

" And yet, how proud I was of the madness! How I loved to say that words were more beautiful than the things for which they stood, and that the names of the world's beautiful women, Sappho, Fiametta, Guinivere, were more beautiful than Sappho, Fiametta, Guinivere themselves; that the names of the stars were lovelier than any star — who has ever found the Pleiades so beautiful as their name, or any king so great as the sound of Orion ? — and what, anywhere in the Universe, is lovely enough to bear Arcturus for its name? —   Ah ! you know how I used to talk — poor fool, poor lover of coloured shadows ! "

" Yes, dear," said Beatrice soothingly, " but that is passed now, and you must not dwell too persistently in the sorrow of it, or in your grief for little Wonder.   That too is to dwell with shadows, and to dwell with shadows either of grief or joy is dangerous for the soul."

" I   know.   But fear not, Beatrice. Perhaps there was the danger of my passing from one cloudland to another — for I never knew how I loved our Wonder till now, and I longed, if only by imagination, to follow her where she has gone, and share with her the life together we have lost here — "

"But that can never be," said Beatrice; "you must accept it, Antony. We shall only meet her again by doing that. The sooner we can say from our hearts 'She is lost here,' the nearer is she to being found in another world. Yes, Antony dear, even Wonder's little shadow must be left behind, if we are to mount together the hills of life."

"My wonderful Beatrice! Yes, the hills of life. No more its woods, but its hills, bathed in a vast and open sunshine. Look around us — how nobly simple is every line and shape! Far below the horizon nature is elaborate, full of fancies, — mazy watercourses, delicate dingles, fantastically gloomy ravines, misshapen woods, gibbering with diablerie; but here how simple, how great, how good she is! There is not a shape subtler than a common bowl, and the colours are alphabetical — and yet, by what taking of thought could she have achieved an effect so grand, at once so beautiful and so holy?"

"Yes, one might call it the good beauty," said Beatrice.

"Yes," continued Antony, perhaps somewhat ominously interested in the subject, "that is a great mystery — the seeming moral meaning of the forms of things. Some shapes, however beautiful, suggest evil; others, however ugly, suggest good. As we look at a snake, or a spider, we know that evil is shaped like that; and not only animate things but inanimate. Some aspects of nature are essentially evil. There are landscapes that injure the soul to look at, there are sunsets that are unholy, there are trees breathing spiritual pestilence as surely as some men breathe it — "

"Do you remember," continued Antony with a smile, which died as he realised he was committed to an allusion best forgotten, "that old twisted tree that stood on the moor near our wood? I often wonder what mysterious sin he had committed — "

" Yes," laughed Beatrice, " he looked a terribly depraved old tree, I must admit — but don't you think that when we have arrived at the discussion of the mysterious sins of trees it is time to start home ? "

" Yes, indeed," said Antony gaily, " let us change the subject to the vices of flowers."

From which conversation it will be seen that Antony's mind was still revolving with unconscious attraction around the mystery of Art. Was it some far-travelled sea-wind bringing faint strains from that sunken harp, strains too subtle for the ear, and even unrecognised by the mind ?

CHAPTER XIX

LAST TALK ON THE HILLS

BEATRICE'S prayer had been answered. Antony had come back to her. She was necessary to him once more. The old look was in his eyes, the old sound in his voice. One day as they were out together she was so conscious of this happiness returned that she could not forbear speaking of it — with an inner feeling that it was better to be happy in silence.

What is that instinct in us which tells us that we risk our happiness in speaking of it? Happiness is such a frightened thing that it flies at the sound of its own name. And yet of what shall we speak if not our happiness? Of our sorrows we can keep silence, but our joys we long to utter.

So Beatrice spoke of her great happiness to Antony, and told him too of her old great unhappiness and her longing for death.

" What a strange and terrible dream it has been — but thank God, we are out in the daylight at last," said Antony.   " O my little Beatrice, to think that I could have forsaken you like that !   Surely if you had come and taken me by the hands and looked deep into my eyes, and called me out of the dream, I must have awakened, for, cruel as it was, the dream was but part of a greater dream, the dream of my love for you — "

" But I understand it all now," he continued, " see it all.   Do you remember saying that perhaps I had never loved anything but images all my life ?   It was quite true.   Since I can remember, when I thought I loved something I was sure to find sooner or later that I loved less the object itself than what I could say about it, and when I had said something beautiful, something I could remember and say over and over to myself, I cared little if the object were removed. The spiritual essence of it seemed to have passed over into my words, and I loved the reincarnation best. Only at last have I awakened to realities, and the shadows flee away. The worshipper of the Image is dead within me. But alas! that little Wonder had to die first — "

" I used to tell myself," he went on, " that human life, however exquisite, without art to eternalise it, was like a rose showering its petals upon the ground. For so brief a space the rose stood perfect, then fell in a ruin of perfume. Wonderful moments had human life, but without art were they not like pearls falling into a gulf? So I said : there is nothing real but art. The material of art passes — human love, human beauty — but art remains. It is the image, not the reality, that is everlasting. I will live in the image."

"But I know now," he once more resumed, " that there is a higher immortality than art's, — the immortality of love. The immortality of art indeed is one of those curious illusions of man's self-love which a moment's thought dispels. Art, who need be told, is as dependent for its survival on the survival of its physical media as man's body itself—and though the epic and the great canvas escape combustion for a million years, they must burn at last, burn with all the other accumulated shadows of time. What we call immortality in art is but the shadow of the soul's immortality ; but the immortality of love is that of the soul itself — "

" O Antony," interrupted Beatrice, " you really believe that now ? You will never doubt it again ? "

" We never doubt what we have really seen, and I had never seen before," answered Antony, taking her hand and looking deep into her eyes, " never seen it as I see it now."

" And you will never doubt it again ? "

" Never."

" Whatever that voice should say to you ? "

" I shall never hear that voice again."

" O Antony, is it really true ? You have come back to me. I can hardly believe it."

" Listen, Beatrice ; when we return to the Valley, return only to leave it for ever, I will take the Image and smash it in a hundred pieces — for I hate it now as much as I once loved it. Fear not ; it will never trouble our peace again."

The mention of the valley was a momentary cloud on Beatrice's happiness, but as she looked into Antony's resolute love-lit face, it melted away.

CHAPTER XX

ANTONY'S JUDGMENT UPON SILENCIEUX

So the weeks and months went by for those two upon the hills, and the soul of Antony grew stronger day by day, and his love with it — and the face of Beatrice was like a bird singing. At last the spring came, and the snow was no more needed to keep warm the flowers. With the flowers came the snowdrop-soul of Wonder, and the thoughts of mother and father turned to the place of kind old trees and tender country bells, where in the unflowering November they had laid her. These dark months the chemic earth had been busy with the little body they loved, and by this time Wonder would be many violets.

"Let us go to Wonder," they said; "she is awake now."

So they went to Wonder, and found her surrounded, in her earth cradle, by a great singing of birds, and blossoms and green leaves innumerable. It was more like a palace than a graveyard, and they went away happy for their little one.

There remained now to take leave of the valley, which indeed looked its loveliest, as though to allure them to remain. Some days they must stay to make the necessary preparations for their departure. Among these, in Antony's mind, the first and most necessary was that destruction of Silencieux which he had promised himself and his wife upon the hills.

The first afternoon Beatrice noted him take a great hammer, and set out up the wood. She gave him a look of love and trust as he went — though there was a secret tremor in her heart, for she knew, perhaps better than he, how strong was the power of Silencieux.

But in Antony's heart was no misgiving, or backsliding. In those months on the hills he had realised human love, in the love of a true and tender and fairy-like woman, and he knew that no illusions, however specious, were worth that reality — a reality with all the magic of an illusion. He gripped the hammer in his hand joyfully, eager to smite featureless the face which had so misled him, brought such tragic sorrow to those he had loved.

Still, for all his unshaken purpose, it was strange to see again the face that had meant so much to him, around which his thoughts had circled consciously or unconsciously all these absent weeks.

Seldom has a face seen again after long separation seemed so disenchanted as Silencieux's. Was this she whom he had worshipped, she who had told him in that strange voice of her immortal lovers, she with whom he had sung by the sea, she with whom he had danced those strange dances in the town, she who had whispered low that awful command, she to whom he had sacrificed his little child?

She was just a dusty, neglected cast — nothing more.

Wonder's voice came back to him: "No, Daddy, they tasted of dust" — and at that thought he gripped the hammer ready to strike.

And yet, even thus, she was a beautiful work of man's hands, and Antony, hating to destroy beauty, still forbore to strike — just as he would have shrunk from breaking in pieces a shapely vase. Then, too, the resemblance to Beatrice took him again. Crudely to smash features so like hers seemed a sort of mimic murder. So he still hesitated. Was there no other way? Then the thought came to him: "Bury her." It pleased him. Yes, he would bury her.

So, having found a spade, he took her from the wall, and looked from his door into the wood, pondering where her grave should be. A whitebeam at a little distance made a vivid conflagration of green amid the sombre boles of the pines. Pinewoods rely on their undergrowth — bracken and whortleberry and occasional bushes — for their spring illuminations, and the whitebeam shone as bright in that wood as a lamp in the dark.

" I will bury her beneath the whitebeam," said Antony, and he carried her thither.

Soon the grave was dug amid the pushing fronds of the young ferns, and taking one long look at her, Antony laid her in the earth, and covered her up from sight. Was it only fancy that as he turned away a faint music seemed to arise from the ground, forming into the word. " Resurgam " as it died away ?

" It is done," said Antony to Beatrice.

" But I could not break her, she looked so like you ; so I buried her in the wood."

Beatrice kissed him gratefully. But her heart would have been more satisfied had Silencieux been broken.

CHAPTER XXI

"RESURGAM !"

" Resurgam ! "

Had his senses deceived him? They must have deceived him. And yet that music at least had seemed startlingly near, sudden, and sweet, as though one should tread upon a harp in the grass. For the next day or two Antony could not get it out of his ears, and often, like a sweet wail through the wood, he seemed to hear the word " Resurgam."

Was Silencieux a living spirit, after all, — no mere illusion, but one of those beautiful demons of evil that do possess the souls of men?

He went and stood by Silencieux's grave. It was just as he had left it. Only an early yellow butterfly stood fanning itself on the freshly turned earth.

Was it the soul of Silencieux?

Cursing himself for a madman, he turned away, but had not gone many yards, when once more — there was that sudden strain of music and the word " Resurgam " somewhere on the wind.

This time he knew he was not mistaken, but to believe it true — O God, he must not believe it true. Reality or fancy, it was an evil thing which he had cast out of his life — and he closed his ears and fled.

Yet, though he loyally strove to quench that music in the sound of Beatrice's voice, deep in his heart he knew that the night would come when he would take his lantern and spade, wearily, as one who at length after hopeless striving obeys once more some imperious weakness — and look on the face of Silencieux again.

Too surely that night came, and, as in a

dream, Antony found himself in the dark
spring night hastening with lantern and
spade to Silencieux's grave. It was only
just to look on her face again, to see if she
really lived like a vampire in the earth;
and were she to be alive, he vowed to kill
her where she lay — for into his life again
he knew she must not come.

As he neared the whitebeam, a gust of
wind blew out his lantern, and he stood in
the profound darkness of the trees. While
he attempted to relight it, he thought
he saw a faint light at the foot of the
whitebeam, as of a radiance welling out
of the earth; but he dismissed it as fancy.

Then, having relit the lantern, he set
the spade into the ground, and speedily
removed the soil from the white face below. As he uncovered it, the wind again
extinguished the lantern, and there, to his
amazement and terror, was the face of
Silencieux shining radiantly in the darkness. The hole in which she lay brimmed

over with light, as a spring wells out of
the hillside. Her face was almost trans-
parent with brightness, and presently she
spoke low, with a voice sweeter than
Antony had ever heard before. It was
the voice of that magic harp at the bottom
of the sea, it was the voice that had told
him of her lovers, the voice of hidden
music that had cried "Resurgam" through
the wood.

"Antony," she said, "sing me songs
of little Wonder."

And, forgetting all but the magic of her
voice, the ecstasy of being hers again,
Antony carried her with him to the châlet,
and setting her in her accustomed place,
gazed at her with his whole soul.

"Sing me songs of little Wonder," she
repeated.

"You bid me sing of little Wonder!"
cried Antony, half in terror of this beautiful evil face that drew him irresistibly as
the moon, "you, who took her from me!"

"Who but I should bid you sing of Wonder?" answered Silencieux. "I loved her. That was why I took her from you, that by your grief she should live for ever. There is no one but I who can give you back your little Wonder — no one but I who can give you back anything you have lost. If you love me faithfully, Antony — there is nothing you can lose, but in me you will find it again."

Antony bowed his head, his heart breaking for Beatrice — but who is not powerless against his own soul?

"Listen," said Silencieux again. "Once on a time there was a beautiful girl who died, and from her grave grew a wonderful flower, which all the world came to see. 'Yet it seems a pity,' said one, 'that so beautiful a girl should have died.' 'Ah,' said a poet standing by, 'there was no other way of making the flower!'"

9

And again, as Antony still kept silence in his agony, Silencieux said, " Listen."

" Listen, Antony. You have hidden yourself away from me, you have put seas and lands between us, you have denied me with bitter curses, you have vowed to thrust me from your life, you have given your allegiance to the warm and pretty humanity of a day, and reviled the august cold marble of immortality. But it is all in vain. In your heart of hearts you love no human thing, you love not even yourself, you love only the eternal spirit of beauty in all things, you love only me. Me you may sacrifice, your own heart you may deny, in the weakness of human pity for human love; but, should this be, your life will be in secret broken, purposeless, and haunted, and to me at last you will come, at the end — at the end and too late. This is your own heart's voice; you know if it be true."

" It is true," moaned Antony.

" Many men and many loves are there in this world," continued Silencieux, "and each knows the way of his own love, nor shall anything turn him from it in the end. Here he may go and thither he may turn, but in the end there is only one way of joy for each, and in that way must he go or perish. Many faces are fair upon the earth, but for each man is a face fairest of all, for which, unless he win it, each must go desolate forever — "

" Face of Eternal Beauty," said Antony, " there is but one face for me for ever. It is yours."

On the morrow Beatrice saw once more that light in Antony's face which made her afraid. He had brought with him some sheets of paper on which were written the songs of little Wonder Silencieux had bidden him sing. They were songs of grief so poignant and beautiful one grew happy in listening to them, and

Antony forgot all in the joy of having made them. He read them to Beatrice in an ecstasy. Her face grew sadder and sadder as he read. When he had finished she said : —

"Antony ! — Silencieux has risen again."

" O Beatrice, Beatrice — I would do anything in the world for you — but I cannot live without her."

CHAPTER XXII

THE STRANGENESS OF ANTONY

FROM this moment Silencieux took possession of Antony as she had never taken it before. Never had he been so inaccessibly withdrawn into his fatal dream. Beatrice forgot her own bitter sorrow in her fear for him, so wrought was he with the fires that consumed him. Some days she almost feared for his reason, and she longed to watch over him, but his old irritation at her presence had returned.

As the summer days came on, she would see him disappear through the green door of the wood at morning and return by it at evening; but all the day each had been alone, Beatrice alone with a solitude in which was now no longer any Wonder.

The summer beauty gave her courage, but she knew that the end could not be very far away.

One day there had been that in Antony's manner which had more than usually alarmed her, and when night fell and he had not returned, she went up the wood in search of him, her heart full of forebodings. As she neared the châlet she seemed to hear voices. No! there was only one voice. Antony was talking to some one. Careful to make no noise, she stole up to the window and looked in. The sight that met her eyes filled her with a great dread. "O God, he is going mad," she cried to herself.

Antony was sitting in a big chair drawn up to the fire. Opposite to him, lying back in her cushions, was the Image draped in a large black velvet cloak. A table stood between them, and on it stood two glasses, and a decanter nearly empty of wine. Silencieux's glass stood untasted, but Antony had evidently been drinking deeply, for his cheeks were flushed and his eyes wild.

He was speaking in angry, passionate, despairing tones. One of her strange moods of silence had come upon Silencieux, and she lay back in her pillows stonily unresponsive.

"For God's sake speak to me," Antony cried. "I love you with my whole heart. I have sacrificed all I love for your sake. I would die for you this instant — yes! a hundred thousand deaths. But you will not answer me one little word —"

But there was no answer.

"Silencieux! Have you ceased to love me? Is the dream once more at an end, the magic faded? Oh, speak — tell me — anything — only speak!" But still Silencieux neither spoke nor smiled.

"Listen, Silencieux," at last cried Antony, beside himself, "unless you answer me, I will die this night, and my blood shall be upon your cruel altar for ever."

As he spoke he snatched a dagger from among some bibelots on his mantel, and drew it from its sheath.

"You are proud of your martyrs," he laughed ; "see, I will bleed to death for your sake. In God's name speak."

But Silencieux spoke nothing at all.

Then Beatrice, watching in terror, seeing by his face that he would really kill himself, ran round to the door and broke in, crying, "O my poor Antony !" but already he had plunged the dagger amid the veins of his left wrist, and was watching the blood gush out with a strange delight.

As Beatrice burst in, he looked up at her, and mistook her for Silencieux.

"Ah !" he said, "you speak at last. You love me now, when it is too late — when I am dying."

As he said this his face grew white and he fainted away.

For many days Antony lay unconscious, racked by terrible delirium. The doctor called it brain fever. It was not the common form, he said, but a more dangerous form, to which only imaginative men were subject. It was a form of madness all the more malignant because the sufferer, and particularly his friends, might go for years without suspecting it. The doctor gave the disease no name.

During his illness Antony spoke to Beatrice all the time as Silencieux, but one day, when he was nearly well again, he suddenly turned upon her in enraged disappointment, with a curious harshness he had never shown before, as though the gentleness of his soul had died during his illness, and exclaimed : —

"Why, you are not Silencieux, after all ! "

"I am Beatrice," said his wife gently ; "Beatrice, who loves you with her whole heart."

" But I love Silencieux — "

Beatrice hid her face and sobbed.

" Where is Silencieux ?   Bring me Silencieux.   I see !   You have taken her away while I was ill — I will go and seek her myself," and he attempted to rise.

" You are too weak.   You must not get up, Antony.   I will bring you Silencieux."

And so, till he was well enough to leave his bed, Silencieux hung facing Antony on his bedroom wall, and on his first walk out into the air, he took her with him and set her once more in her old shrine in the wood.

Now, by this time, the heart of Beatrice was broken.

CHAPTER XXIII

BEATRICE FULFILS HER DESTINY

THE heart of Beatrice was broken, and there was now no use or place for her in the world. Wonder was gone, and Antony was even further away. She knew now that he would never come back to her. Never again could return even the illusion of those happy weeks on the hills. Antony would be hers no more for ever.

There but remained for her to fulfil her destiny, the destiny she had vaguely known ever since Antony had brought home the Image, and shown her how the Seine water had moulded the hair and made wet the eyelashes.

For some weeks now Beatrice had been living on the border of another world. She had finally abandoned all her hopes of earthly joy — and to Antony she was no longer any help or happiness. He had needed her again for a few brief weeks, but now he needed her no more. His every look told her how he wished her out of his life. And she had no one else in the world.

But in another world she had her little Wonder. Lately she had begun to meet her in the lanes. In the day she wore garlands of flowers round her head, and in the night a great light. She would go to meet her at night, that the light might lead her steps.

So one night while Antony banqueted strangely with Silencieux, she drew her cloak around her and stole up the wood, to look a last good-bye at him as he sat laughing with his shadows.

" Good-bye, Antony, good-bye," she cried. " I had but human love to give you. I surrender you to the love of the divine."

Then noting how full of blossom were the lanes, and how sweet was the night air, and smitten through all her senses with the song and perfume of the world she was about to leave, she found her way, with a strange gladness of release, to the Three Black Ponds.

It was moonlight, and the dwarf oak-trees made druid shadows all along the leafy galleries that overhung the pools. The pools themselves shone with a start-ling silver — so hushed, so dreamy was all that surrounded them that there seemed something of an unnatural wakefulness, a daylight observation, in their brilliant surfaces, — and on them, as last year, the lilies floated like the crowns of sunken queens. But the third pool lay more in shadow, and by that, as it seemed to Bea-trice, a light was shining.

Yes, a light was shining and a voice was calling. " Mother," it called, " little Mother. I am waiting for you. Here, little Mother. Here by the water-lilies we could not gather."

Beatrice, following the voice, stepped along the causeway and sank among the lilies; and as she sank she seemed to see Antony bending over the pond, saying: "How beautiful she looks, how beautiful, lying there among the lilies!"

On the morrow, when they had drawn Beatrice from the pond, with lilies in her hair, Antony bent over her and said:—

"It is very sad—Poor little Beatrice—but how beautiful! It must be wonderful to die like that."

And then again he said: "She is strangely like Silencieux."

Then he walked up the wood, in a great serenity of mind. He had lost Wonder, but she lived again in his songs. He had lost Beatrice, but he had her image—did she not live for ever in Silencieux?

So he went up the wood, whistling

softly to himself — but lo ! when he opened his châlet door, there was a strange light in the room. The eyes of Silencieux were wide open, and from her lips hung a dark moth with the face of death between his wings.

THE END